Proud 123

Spring Sprouts

Spring Sprouts

JUDY DELTON

Illustrated by Alan Tiegreen

A YEARLING BOOK

Published by
Bantam Doubleday Dell Books for Young Readers
a division of
Bantam Doubleday Dell Publishing Group, Inc.
1540 Broadway
New York, New York 10036

The trademarks Yearling® and Dell® are registered in the U.S. Patent and Trademark Office and in other countries.

ISBN: 0-440-40160-7

Printed in the United States of America

April 1989

20   19   18   17   16   15   14   13

CWO

For Goose's Friend, and mine, Heron Gardner

Contents

1 Seeds   1

2 The Dandelion Deed   13

3 Talking to Radishes   22

4 Cows and Sows   33

5 The Yolk on Roger   44

6 No Badge for Molly   56

7 It's a Monster!   65

CHAPTER 1

Seeds

"What is cowhide used for the most?" Roger White asked Molly Duff.

Molly sighed. Roger had gotten *Jake's Joke Book* for his birthday. All he did was ask the Pee Wee Scouts riddles.

"Shoes," said Molly. "Cowhide is used for shoes."

Roger shook his head. "You don't know, do you?" he shouted. "Guess again!"

"Belts," said Lisa Ronning. "My uncle has a cowhide belt."

"Nope," said Roger.

"Tepees," said Sonny Betz. "Tepees are made of cowhide."

1

"No they aren't," said Roger. "They're made of canvas. Or plastic or something."

"Not Indian tepees," said Sonny.

"Well, that's not the answer," said Roger.

Roger was jumping up and down. "Do you know, Mrs. Peters?" he asked.

"The main use for cowhide," said Mrs. Peters slowly, "is to hold a cow together."

Roger didn't laugh. He began to pout. He didn't like it when someone knew the punch line.

"I'm sorry," said Mrs. Peters, with a smile. "But I heard that joke on the radio this morning."

The Pee Wee Scouts were in Mrs. Peters's backyard. It was a hot spring day. The sun poured down on Molly's head. It made her hair hot.

"We can get sunburned out here," said her friend Mary Beth Kelly.

"I thought it would be fun to have our meeting outside today," said Mrs. Peters. She was the Pee Wee Scout troop leader. "Winter was so long and cold. Spring feels good. The sun is good for Nick."

Nick was Mrs. Peters's brand-new baby. He was only four months old. He sat in his stroller. The Scouts were giving him rides around the yard.

"I mentioned the sun," said Mrs. Peters, "because we are going to talk about vitamins today. And the sun has vitamin D in it."

Some of the Scouts groaned.

"Yuck," said Tracy Barnes. "I don't like vitamins. Vegetables have them. Like spinach."

"Vitamins are in lots of things," said Mrs. Peters. "Lots of good things. Even ice cream."

Molly rubbed her stomach. Ice cream

would taste good right now, she thought. Cold and creamy. Yum.

"I'd like to sit in a barrel of ice cream right now," said Kevin Moe. "Right up to my neck."

The Pee Wees laughed. It was a funny thing to picture. Kevin in a tub of ice cream.

Mrs. Peters walked over to the picnic table. She was carrying a big basket. She dumped it out on the table.

Ker-plunk.

Lots of little packages fell out.

Pop, pop, pop.

Brightly colored little packages.

The Scouts looked at the packages.

Red and green and blue.

Yellow and pink and lilac.

Everyone sat down on the benches around the table. Mrs. Peters propped Nick up so he could see.

"What are they?" asked Tracy. She shook one of the little packages. It sounded noisy. Like little beads were inside.

Rattle, rattle, rattle.

"I know what they are," said Rachel Meyers. "Seeds!"

"You're right," said Mrs. Peters. "They are seeds to plant in gardens."

She opened one of the little packages. Little tiny dots were inside.

"From these little seeds," said their leader, "come big fat radishes!"

"How can they?" asked Tim. He looked like he didn't believe her.

"That's nothing," said Rachel. "A great big tree grows from just a little seed."

The Pee Wees looked at the tree overhead. It was huge. Little green leaves were coming out. Light-green leaves.

"That didn't come from a little seed," scoffed Tim.

"Did too," said Rachel. "Didn't it, Mrs. Peters?"

"It came from an acorn," said Mrs. Peters. "An acorn is a seed too."

Rachel made a face at Tim.

"But these seeds," said Mrs. Peters, shaking a package, "are for radishes and carrots. I thought it would be fun for all of you to plant your very own garden while we study vitamins. Spring is the time to plant gardens."

"I love to dig in the dirt," said Sonny.

"Me too," said Kenny Baker.

"My dad plants a garden every spring," said Rachel. "My mom freezes the vegetables."

"Then maybe you already know how to do it," said Mrs. Peters. "Rachel can help us."

Mrs. Peters passed a little packet of seeds to each Scout.

"First you find a nice sunny spot and dig up the dirt," Mrs. Peters explained. "Then you rake it smooth."

She walked over to a little place in the yard that was already dug and raked. "Mr. Peters got this ready last night," she said.

She bent down and put a ruler on the ground. She made a little ditch alongside it with a knife. "This is so the row will be nice and straight," she said.

Then she sprinkled the seeds along the ruler, into the little ditch.

"Don't plant them too deep," she said. "And not too close together. Every day you must water your garden. Water and sun will make it grow."

Molly couldn't wait to get home and plant her seeds. She wanted to have the very first radish. And the biggest one of all.

"This hot sun will bring them up fast," said Mrs. Peters. She washed her hands off under the outdoor faucet.

Then everyone sat down at the table again.

"Besides the garden," she said, "we will keep vitamin scrapbooks."

She held up a big picture of a carrot. "This has lots of vitamin A."

Then she held up a picture of a lemon. "This has lots of vitamin C. You can cut pictures out of old magazines. After you make your scrapbooks and plant your gardens, we will talk about nutrition. Then you will earn your EAT RIGHT badges."

The Pee Wees cheered, "Yeah!"

It was fun to plant a garden. And make scrapbooks. And it was even more fun to get a new badge!

"We've got a seed catalog at home,"

said Lisa. "I can find lots of vegetables in that."

Mrs. Peters talked some more about vitamins and nutrition. About what to eat for breakfast, for instance.

Roger raised his hand. "Can I tell a joke?" he said.

"Yes," said Mrs. Peters.

"What are two things you can't eat for breakfast?" he said.

The Scouts thought about the question.

"Steak," said Molly.

"An ice-cream soda," said Patty.

Roger shook his head. "Lunch and dinner!" he shouted.

"Boo!" said all the Scouts together.

Roger looked embarrassed.

Then they all joined hands and sang the Pee Wee Scout song. And they said the Pee Wee Scout pledge.

Molly loved the Scout meetings.

But she wanted to hurry home.
To plant her garden.
Molly wanted to be the first one to get her little packet of seeds in the ground.

CHAPTER 2

The Dandelion Deed

After supper Molly's dad showed her where she could plant a garden.

"The sun will be there every morning," said Mr. Duff.

Molly raked the garden. Then she made straight lines with a ruler just as Mrs. Peters had. She put in a little fertilizer that her dad had given her.

Mrs. Peters hadn't talked about fertilizer. Maybe it was a secret trick. To make the seeds grow. To get the badge faster.

Molly hoped it wasn't cheating.

Molly dropped the seeds along the ruler.

Nice and straight. Not too deep. Not too close together.

Then she covered the seeds with a little dirt and patted them down.

Pat, pat, pat.

"Grow fast," she said to the seeds. She watered them with the hose.

Now I have to wait, she thought. Hurry up and wait. She stared at the smooth dirt for a long time. Then she went inside.

* * *

Every morning before school Molly ran out to look at her garden. Every morning it looked the same.

Flat and black.

Ants crawled over it.

Angleworms crawled through it.

But nothing else happened.

After school one day Molly and Mary Beth and Lisa looked for pictures for their scrapbooks. They looked through magazines for pictures of fruits and vegetables.

The girls were on Mary Beth's front porch. It was another warm spring day.

"Here's spaghetti," said Lisa.

"Spaghetti isn't a fruit or vegetable," said Molly. "It doesn't even grow in a garden."

"So, I can still use it," said Lisa. She started to cut it out. It looked so good.

"Yum," said Lisa. "I want spaghetti in my book."

"You can't," said Molly. "What would you put under it, vitamin S?"

The girls laughed.

Down the street they saw Roger coming toward them. He was riding on his bike.

"Hey," he said when he got close. He dragged his feet and came to a stop. "What's the difference between a new penny and an old dime?" he asked.

"You told us last week," said Mary Beth. "Nine cents."

"Oh, yeah. I forgot," said Roger. "I'll go tell Patty. She'll laugh at anything I say."

He rode on down the street.

On Tuesday Mrs. Peters asked, "Is anyone's garden up yet?"

Rachel waved her hand. "Mine is, Mrs.

Peters! My radishes have little green leaves!"

"How could yours come up so fast?" asked Molly.

"My dad started seeds in the house a month ago," Rachel admitted. "Then we put them outside."

"That's cheating," whispered Tracy. "She got a head start."

"They aren't even her own radishes," whispered Lisa.

"Keep your eyes on your gardens," said Mrs. Peters. "Water them every day. This hot weather will bring your seeds up fast."

Then the Pee Wee Scouts shared their scrapbooks. They held up the pictures of the brightly colored vegetables.

"I can't find any beans," said Patty.

"I can't find anything with vitamin C," said Tim.

"C is easy," said Kenny. "Oranges have

17

vitamin C. There are lots of pictures of oranges."

Molly tried to remember that. If orange began with a *c*, it would be easier.

After the scrapbooks were put away, the Pee Wee Scouts told about the good deeds they had done during the past week.

"I mowed the yard with my dad," said Roger. "We filled about a zillion garbage bags with grass."

"I painted the fence in our yard," said Patty.

"Me too," said Kenny, Patty's twin brother. "We painted together."

It would be fun to be a twin, thought Molly. Molly was an only child.

Tim was waving his hand.

"Yes, Tim," said Mrs. Peters.

"I picked dandelion leaves for supper," he said.

The Scouts snickered. They made gag-
ging noises.

"Yuck!" said Rachel.

"Gross," said Kevin.

Mrs. Peters held up her hand. "Dandelion greens make a good salad," she said.
"And they can be cooked too. They are
loaded with vitamins. Tim did a good

deed. And he found a new vegetable for his scrapbook."

"I'm going to pick dandelions tonight," said Rachel.

"So am I, we've got lots," said Tracy. "I'll bring some next week."

"It's Tim's good deed," said Mrs. Peters. "I think we should let Tim have the dandelion deed."

Then Mrs. Peters added, "Next week I have a surprise for you. Be here right on time. Wear jeans. That's all I'm going to tell you."

"Are we going to the zoo?" asked Kevin.

"Is it another Pee Wee weenie roast?" shouted Roger.

Mrs. Peters held up her hand. She smiled. "It's a surprise," she said.

They sang their Pee Wee Scout song.

They said their Pee Wee Scout pledge.

But all they could think about was the surprise. Molly hoped the week would go fast. She was so curious!

"Knock, knock," said Roger as the Scouts left.

"Knock, knock!" he said more loudly.

"Who's there?" said Patty.

"Ether," said Roger.

"Ether who?" said Patty.

"Ether Bunny!" Roger roared. "It's an Easter joke, get it? Ether bunny?"

"Easter is over," said Rachel.

"So?" said Roger. "It's still funny."

But the Scouts had other things on their minds. Things like seeds and scrapbooks and surprises.

Mostly surprises!

CHAPTER 3

Talking to Radishes

After school, Wednesday, Molly ran home to check her garden. Nothing yet. She stamped her foot. When would those radishes come up?

On Thursday Kevin ran all the way to school. Some Pee Wee Scouts were outside talking together.

"My garden's up!" he shouted, out of breath. "My carrots are growing."

"Great," said Mary Beth.

"You're the first one," said Patty. "Except Rachel."

Molly felt angry. If she couldn't be first, she at least wanted to be second.

Lisa and Tracy looked mad too. They didn't look happy for Kevin.

At noon the Scouts walked by Kevin's house on their way home to lunch. He took them into his backyard.

"I don't see anything," said Tim.

"Right here," said Kevin, getting down on the ground and pointing.

Molly got down on her knees. She squinted. She got very close to the ground. She could see something very little. Something barely there. Barely green.

"It's them!" boasted Kevin. "It's my carrots!"

"You can't see them when you stand up," said Rachel.

Kevin didn't care. He knew they were there.

On Sunday it was very hot. In the evening Molly watered her radishes.

Her grandma said plants like it when you talk to them. Molly tried it. She told the radishes to hurry up and grow.

"Come on, little radishes," Molly said. "You have lots of water and lots of sun. I need you to get my badge. Please grow big and fat." Molly got down on the ground. "Please, please, please!" she said.

The garden didn't answer.

But Molly's next-door neighbor did! Mrs. Berry was shaking a dust mop. She called to Molly, "Did you say something?"

Molly shook her head. "I was talking to my garden," she said.

"Come and talk to mine too," said Mrs. Berry. "Only my rhubarb is up so far."

Molly ducked into the house. Mrs. Berry was laughing at her. Molly felt silly.

At last, on Tuesday morning before school, when Molly looked at her garden something was there! Something green! "My radishes!" she screamed to her mother. "My radishes are up!"

"Good for you!" said Mrs. Duff.

They were barely up, but they were there. Tiny thin green leaves. It was good that I talked to them, Molly thought. And watered them. Just in time too. They grew on Pee Wee Scout day.

Molly ran all the way to school. She bounced in her seat all day waiting for three o'clock.

She didn't want to read.

She didn't want to subtract.

She didn't want to draw pictures.

She wanted to tell Mrs. Peters that her garden was growing!

At recess the other Scouts weren't

interested in gardens. "I wonder what our surprise is," said Lisa.

Molly had almost forgotten about the surprise.

"I'll bet it's a picnic," said Kenny. Kenny liked picnics.

"I know what it is," boasted Sonny. "Because my mom is the assistant Scout leader."

"That isn't fair," said Tracy.

"Your mom shouldn't tell you Scout secrets," muttered Molly.

"Why not?" said Sonny.

"Because it's not fair," said Mary Beth. "Molly's right."

"Yeah," said Molly, but Sonny knew the secret anyway.

Sonny had overalls on. "Because of the surprise," he said.

At three o'clock the Scouts rushed out of the school. They dashed to Mrs.

Peters's. Molly was all out of breath when they got there.

"My garden is up!" she blurted out.

"So is mine," said Mary Beth.

"Mine too," said Lisa.

"Wonderful!" said Mrs. Peters, throwing her hands into the air in excitement. "I told you it would be soon!"

"Mine isn't up," said Tim.

"Maybe you planted the seeds deeper, Tim. It will just take a little longer then."

Then Mrs. Peters said, "Now that so many gardens are up, we will all wait to see who brings in the first radish and the first carrot."

Molly jumped up and down thinking about that. She was going to talk to her radishes every day. And water them. Soak them. Drown them. They liked water, and she would give them plenty.

"Now!" said Mrs. Peters. "Today is our surprise!"

Mrs. Betz was there. She had overalls on too.

She and Sonny looked like twins.

A baby-sitter was there too. To take care of Nick. The Scouts sat like statues, waiting for the news.

"Today," said Mrs. Peters, "we are going to visit a dairy farm."

Roger put his fingers in his mouth and gave a long whistle. Then he frowned. "You mean Dairy Queen?" he asked.

"No, a dairy farm," said Mrs. Peters. "Where cows are raised for their milk. The cows give milk and the milk is sold to a milk company and the milk company sells it to stores. First it is sterilized and pasteurized and put into cartons. Some is made into cheese and ice cream. Then your parents buy it."

Molly began to get hungry. Ice-cold milk would be good now. Or ice cream. Maybe they would have ice cream at the dairy farm.

"Milk gives us lots of calcium," Mrs. Peters went on. "For strong bones. So you can run and play and lift things."

Roger flexed his muscles. "I drink lots of milk," he said. "I've got lots of calcium."

"So do I," said Tim.

"I've got more," said Roger.

"I've got more calcium than all of you," said Kevin, bending his arms and flexing his muscles.

Rachel was waving her hand.

"Mrs. Peters," she called. "Calcium is good for your teeth too. My dad says so. He's a dentist."

"Milk is very important in our diet," agreed Mrs. Peters. "I thought it would be fun to see where it comes from."

Molly liked to go on trips. She didn't care where they went. It would be fun to ride on the bus out into the country. Hey, that's why Sonny and Mrs. Betz were wearing overalls, thought Molly. They dressed like farmers who work in a barn.

Molly wanted to be the first one on the bus. She would save a seat for her best friend, Mary Beth.

"Let's remember our manners," Mrs. Peters was saying. "And learn as much about dairy farms as we can."

"Moooo," said Molly.

"Moooo back," said Kevin.

It was time for the surprise to begin.

CHAPTER 4

Cows and Sows

On the way to the farm, Roger told jokes.

"If an elephant sits on a fence, what time is it?" he said.

"Noon," said Tracy.

Roger shook his head. "Wrong," he said.

"An elephant can't sit on a fence," said Rachel. "He'd fall off."

"What time? What time?" shouted Roger. "Give up?"

At last the Pee Wees gave up.

"Time to get a new fence!" said Roger. "Get it?"

Most of the Scouts groaned. But Roger laughed out loud.

Patty giggled a little bit.

"Look!" shouted Lisa. "Cows!"

As the bus rumbled down the road, the Scouts could see cows.

They could see some baby calves too. Grazing in the pastures.

"Moooo," said Rachel. "Moooo."

"Moooo," said the cows back to her.

"They're answering you," said Mrs. Peters.

"Hey, Rachel talks cow talk!" shouted Roger. "Big-cow Rachel!"

Rachel got up and punched Roger on the arm.

"I am not," she said. Her face got red. The redder it got, the more Roger teased.

"Rachel is a moo-cow!" he chanted. Before long Tim and Kevin joined him.

Rachel went back to her seat. She sat

very quietly. Molly could see tears in Rachel's eyes. No one else noticed.

"Are these the cows we are going to visit?" asked Tracy.

"Not yet," said Mrs. Peters. "The dairy farm has more cows than this. Hundreds of cows."

The bus went up one hill. And down another. "There it is!" called Mrs. Peters. "There is the dairy farm."

"Barns are supposed to be red," said Kenny.

But this barn was not red. It was gray. And it was not barn-shaped. It was long and low. And huge.

"Look at those tall castles!" shouted Tim.

"Those aren't castles," said Mrs. Betz. She laughed. "They are called silos. Corn and feed for the cows are kept in those for the winter. The farmers grow corn all summer and fill up the silos every fall."

The bus pulled into the farmyard. A sign said ROLLY'S DAIRY FARM.

Mr. Rolly came out of a farmhouse to meet them. "Welcome to the dairy farm," he said. He had a round face and a round belly. His overalls were faded. His boots were a little crusty.

The Scouts tumbled off the bus and shook his hand.

Roger was still chanting, "Cow-talk Rachel. Moo-moo. Cow-talk Rachel."

Mr. Rolly began to tell the Scouts about dairy farming. About how they milked the cows and sent the milk to town each day.

But Molly kept watching Rachel. She felt sorry for her. It was no fun to be called a cow.

"Let's go down to the barn," said Mr. Rolly.

Lots of people worked on the farm.

Some were out in the fields planting corn. Some were in the barn with the cows.

"Have you got any other animals?" asked Sonny politely.

"Oh, we've got a sow and some babies," he said. "And some chickens we keep for eggs."

"What's a sow?" asked Lisa.

"A sow is a mother pig," replied Mrs. Peters.

"That's a funny name for a pig," chuckled Tim.

Now Roger had a new chant. He snuck up behind Rachel. "Sow-cow! Sow-cow!" he sang.

Rachel ran behind a haystack and began to cry. Molly followed her.

"He's mean," cried Rachel. "I hate him. I'm not a cow. Or a sow. My mom says I'm small and dainty."

"He didn't mean that you're fat," said

Molly. "He just likes to tease you. Because you get so mad."

"I hate him! I want to go home!" said Rachel. She sniffled.

Molly wondered what to do. She couldn't tell the others that Roger hurt Rachel. Then they'd think Molly was a snitcher.

"Come on," she urged Rachel. "Let's go back."

But Rachel stayed behind the haystack.

Molly wondered if she should give Roger a big shove. He deserved it!

When Molly went back to the group, Roger was telling chicken jokes.

"What is one egg too many?" he asked.

The Scouts ignored him.

"Give up?" he called. "Eggstra! Get it? Eggstra!"

But the Scouts didn't laugh. They followed Mr. Rolly. And listened to the facts about the dairy farm.

"The cows are getting ready to be milked," said Mr. Rolly.

"This isn't like my grandpa's barn," said Mary Beth. "My grandpa's barn smells icky."

"This barn is very clean," said Mrs. Betz.

The cows stood in rows.

Miles of cows.

Cow after cow.

Black-and-white cows.

Each one stood in a little stall of its own. All of the cows were chewing.

"What are they eating?" asked Sonny.

"They're just chewing their cud," said Mr. Rolly, laughing.

"Cows always chew," explained Mrs. Betz.

Molly watched the cows. Their big brown eyes looked at her as she watched. She kept watching. They kept chewing.

40

"Don't walk too close to them," warned Mr. Rolly. "A cow could kick, or swish you with her tail."

"Look at him." Sonny pointed. "Look at that guy! He's got pipes coming out of him."

"Not him," explained Mrs. Betz. "Cows are girls."

"All of them?" said Tracy in surprise. "Why aren't there any boys?"

"Because boys don't give milk," said Mrs. Peters. "These are dairy cows."

Rachel came back. Her eyes looked red. "Girls are better than boys," she said.

"They are not, are they, Mrs. Peters?" asked Kenny.

"Well, they are better on a dairy farm," answered Mrs. Peters, laughing.

Kenny and the other boys raced around the barn. They shouted, "Boy cows! Boy cows! We want boy cows!"

"The bull's out in the pasture," said Mr. Rolly, pointing. "He's the only boy on the farm. And he's mean!"

"All boys are mean," said Rachel to Molly. But she was looking at Roger.

"Uh, oh," said Molly.

Rachel was about to start crying again.

CHAPTER 5

The Yolk on Roger

"**W**hat are those things on the cows' stomachs?" asked Lisa.

"Those are milking machines," said Mrs. Peters. "Farmers used to milk cows by hand, but now farms are too big for them to do that."

"And the milk company inspects the equipment," said Mr. Rolly.

He showed the Scouts how the machines were attached to the cows.

"Like a vacuum-cleaner hose!" squealed Patty. "Oooh, does it hurt them?"

"No, that's the way they work." Mr. Rolly laughed. "With suction."

Pop, pop, pop. Mr. Rolly put the machine on the cow.

"It looks like it hurts," Sonny argued.

Mr. Rolly shook his head. "They like it," he said, patting one of the cows on the head. "That's their job, to give milk. This is Bessie."

Bessie turned her head and looked at Molly. She had huge brown eyes. She was chewing. Chew, chew, chew.

"She looks happy," said Lisa.

"Milk used to go into a pail. Now it goes right into a sterile tank," Mrs. Betz explained.

The Scouts walked up and down looking at the cows and the machines. It was quiet in the barn. Only the sound of cows chewing. And machines humming. It was cool. Cool and clean.

When the Pee Wees had seen all of the cows, Mr. Rolly took them around and showed them the tanks with milk in them. He took some paper cups and filled them with milk.

"This is the freshest milk you'll ever drink," he said.

"Fresh calcium," said Mrs. Betz.

Mr. Rolly handed every Scout a cup.

Molly tasted it. It was warm!

Rachel was going to say yuck! But she changed her mind. Mrs. Peters had warned the Scouts to be polite.

So Rachel just made a face.

"It's hot!" shouted Tim.

"That's because it's right from the cow," said Mr. Rolly. "It hasn't had a chance to chill in the tanks yet."

"It's creamy," said Roger. He finished his and Mr. Rolly handed him another. He was the only Scout who liked warm milk.

Just then Mrs. Rolly came to the door

of the barn with a plate of hot cookies. She was round too. But not as round as Mr. Rolly. She had yellow hair pulled back in a bun.

The Scouts went outside and sat on the thick green grass. They ate the cookies.

"Hey," said Roger, "what happens if an egg falls on your head?"

The Scouts groaned.

"The yolk's on you!" said Roger. "Yolk! Get it?"

"We get it," said Kenny. He rolled his eyes.

Molly laughed a little to herself, even if she was mad at Roger. He told some pretty funny jokes.

"I'd like to live on a farm," said Molly to Mary Beth. "I could have a great big garden then. Lots of radishes!"

"I'd grow watermelons," said Mary Beth. "Like this."

She put her arms out in a big circle to show how big they'd be. "Nice and juicy too."

"Yum," said Molly. "I'd have a pet cow. I'd ride on her back!"

Molly lay down on the green grass. She looked at the sky. The sun was moving toward the west. It was very peaceful on a farm.

"Well," said Mrs. Peters, getting to her feet. "We have been here a long time. It is time to start for home."

She and Mrs. Betz counted Scouts. Mrs. Betz frowned. "There are only ten Scouts here," she said. "I don't see Sonny."

The Scouts looked around. Mrs. Betz was right. Sonny was gone!

"I just saw Sonny a minute ago," said Mrs. Peters.

Mrs. Betz dashed back into the barn. "Sonny! Sonny!" she called.

She ran up and down the rows of cows. She looked in all the stalls. "He's not in there," she cried when she came running out.

"We'll find him!" shouted Roger. "Let's all split up and look in different directions."

"That dumb Sonny," muttered Lisa. "He's always in trouble."

The Pee Wee Scouts spread out.

They looked behind the farmhouse.

They looked in the garage.

And in the shed.

They called his name over and over. "Sonny! Sonny! Son-neee!"

But no one answered.

"What's behind those trees?" Molly asked Lisa.

"Let's look," Lisa said.

They ran down a hill to a clump of trees. Soon the girls reached the other side of the little woods. "Hey!" shouted Molly. "There's Sonny!"

He was standing beside an animal pen. "Baby pigs!" he said smiling.

Soon everyone came running down the hill. Mrs. Betz looked relieved to see Sonny.

"I found the sow," said Sonny proudly.

"Look at those cute baby pigs!" said Lisa. "Their tails are so curly. And they're so pudgy!"

"Just like Rachel," said Roger. "Oink, oink."

Rachel turned and walked away. Her head was down. Molly had to do something about Roger. He was hurting Rachel's feelings too much.

The Scouts tried to reach in between the slats on the fence. They tried to pet the baby pigs.

"Look out!" said Mr. Rolly. "The sow is fussy about her babies."

"Hey! Look at me!" shouted Roger. He had climbed up on top of the fence of the pigpen.

It was narrow.

It was high.

Roger put one foot in front of the other like a tightrope walker.

Rachel wasn't looking, Molly noticed. She was sitting on the grass with her head in her hands. Feeling bad.

Just as Molly started to say something to her, the Scouts heard a shriek.

"Yow-ee!" cried Roger. His left foot slipped from the fence. His arms waved in the air. "Ooooh!" he yelled. "Help!"

Splat!

Everyone ran to the fence.

"Oh, no!" shouted Kevin. "He fell in! Roger fell in the pigpen!"

The Scouts were so surprised they didn't know if they should feel sorry for Roger or laugh. There he was, in the mud!

Roger was covered from head to toe with guck and gook. He had mud all over his arms. And his legs. Even in his hair.

"Quick!" called Mr. Rolly. "Climb out of there before the sow comes after you. She'll think you're after her babies."

"I don't want her babies!" shouted Roger. "Just get me out of here!"

The Pee Wees didn't laugh. They were afraid of the big sow.

But when Rachel saw Roger covered with mud and slime, she began to laugh loudly. She laughed harder and harder!

She pointed at Roger and said, "Ha, look who's the pig now!" She couldn't stop laughing.

Mr. Rolly reached in and pulled Roger over the fence.

"You smell as bad as you look," said Rachel. "You stink!"

Roger looked sheepish. He tried to pretend it was a good joke. But it didn't work.

"The yolk's on you this time," said Rachel. "The yolk's on you!"

Rachel had tears in her eyes, Molly noticed. She was laughing and crying at the same time!

CHAPTER 6

No Badge for Molly

Mr. Rolly led Roger to the barn. He turned on the hose and sprayed Roger all over. But all the dirt did not come off. Only part of it.

"My hair is stiff," said Roger. "And these are my new pants! My mom will kill me."

Mrs. Peters and Mrs. Betz tried to wipe Roger off. But they just smeared the mud. On his skin. On his clothes. On his shoes.

The Pee Wees held their noses.

"Yuck!" said Tim. "You smell like the pigpen."

At last Mrs. Peters herded all the children toward the bus. "We have to get back to town," she said. "It is getting late."

The Scouts thanked the Rollys and got onto the bus.

Molly sat with Rachel.

Mary Beth sat with Lisa.

Roger sat alone.

He did not tell jokes. He wasn't laughing and talking. He just sat and looked out the window.

"Something sure smells in this bus," said Tracy.

Even the bus driver was holding his nose.

"I don't think Roger will call you names anymore," said Molly to Rachel.

"My mom will say that he got a taste of his own medicine," said Rachel. She laughed.

Molly felt relieved that Rachel didn't feel hurt anymore.

At Mrs. Peters's house everyone piled off the bus and started walking home.

"Whew!" said Rachel. "Fresh air!"

*   *   *

All week long the Scouts worked on their scrapbooks. And they watered their gardens.

At the next meeting the Scouts shared their scrapbooks. Mrs. Peters talked more about vitamins and nutrition.

Roger did not smell bad anymore. He went up to Rachel and told her a private joke. "What did the ghost eat for breakfast?" he asked.

When Rachel shook her head, he said, "Scream of wheat!"

Rachel laughed hard.

"Now," said Mrs. Peters. "All you need for your badge is to bring something from your garden."

"I am going to get my badge next week," said Rachel after the meeting.

Molly didn't answer. She was hoping her garden had grown.

*   *   *

At home, Molly sprinkled some fertilizer on her radishes. She weeded them and talked to them and gave them more water.

"Grow, little radishes," she said.

The plants were getting tall. Tall and green. They looked healthy. But Molly couldn't find any radishes on them. Not a single one.

On the way to Mrs. Peters's house, Rachel carried a plastic bag. A red radish was in the bag. Big and red. She held it up. "From my very own garden!" said Rachel.

Molly wanted to grab the bag and hide it. Or grab it and take the big radish for her own. It was the biggest radish Molly had ever seen. Huge. Round like a ball.

"Look, Mrs. Peters!" called Rachel as they went into the house.

"Boys and girls, look at this!" said Mrs. Peters. "It looks like Rachel is the first one to get her new badge! She has a green thumb."

Mrs. Peters got out her camera. She took a picture of Rachel with her big radish. Then she gave Rachel a badge.

It said EAT RIGHT on it. In the middle was a big orange carrot. With green leaves.

Molly thought Rachel should help her out. She had tried to help Rachel at the dairy farm. Rachel should help Molly make her garden grow! Fair is fair.

But Rachel didn't help. And the next Tuesday all the Scouts brought something from their garden. Even Tim. Tim had a little baby carrot. But it was enough for him to get his badge.

Mrs. Peters passed out badges to everyone.

To everyone but Molly.

"Are you watering your garden every day, Molly?" asked Mrs. Peters.

Molly just nodded.

Soon it was time to sing the Pee Wee Scout song.

And say the Pee Wee Scout pledge.

Molly stood in the circle, but she didn't sing or speak. She just moved her lips. Sometimes it was very hard to be a good Scout.

At home, Molly went into the kitchen for a glass of milk. Mrs. Duff was not home yet.

Molly saw something on the counter. It was a little plastic bag with radishes in it! From the grocery store.

Molly looked at them. Round, clean, red radishes. She could take one. She could take one to Scouts and tell Mrs. Peters it was from her garden. Her mom wouldn't know. She didn't count radishes. She just sliced them into the salad.

Molly stared at the bag.

But just as she was about to tear the bag open, her mother came into the kitchen. She thought Molly wanted a vegetable for a snack! "Pretty soon you'll be eating things out of your own garden," said Mrs. Duff. "Won't that be wonderful?"

Molly popped the radish into her mouth. She made a face. It was hot! Radishes were spicy. "Oh, oh!" she said, and she spit it out into the sink.

"Just take one small bite next time," said Mrs. Duff, washing the radishes. She put them in a glass of cold water. "Water makes them crisp," she said.

"I hate radishes!" cried Molly. "They're dumb!"

Mrs. Duff looked surprised as Molly ran out of the kitchen.

CHAPTER 7

It's a Monster!

"What vegetable has vitamin A and is good for your eyes?" asked Roger at the Pee Wee Scout meeting on Tuesday.

"Broccoli," said Mary Beth.

"Beans?" said Kenny.

Roger shook his head. "Give up?"

"Peaches?" said Tim.

"Ho, ho," said Roger.

"Peaches are fruit," said Rachel.

"Give up? Give up?" Roger jumped up and down.

The Pee Wees gave up.

"Carrots!" blurted out Roger proudly.

"You never saw Bugs Bunny with glasses on, did you?"

The Scouts groaned.

"That's a good nutrition joke, Roger," said Mrs. Peters, laughing.

"Thank you," said Roger.

All the Pee Wees were wearing their new EAT RIGHT badges.

All except Molly.

"Any good deeds to report this week?" asked Mrs. Peters.

Hands went up.

"How come you don't have your badge yet?" whispered Lisa to Molly.

"I don't want one," Molly lied.

"You do too," said Mary Beth. "You must have radishes by now. Did you pull them up and look?"

"Pull them up?" repeated Molly.

Mary Beth nodded. "Pull them up and see how big they are," she said. "Knock the dirt off. Some of mine are real little, but some are big. I had to pull up all of them to find the biggest one."

"No kidding?" said Molly. She stood up and said, "I'll be right back," to Mrs. Peters.

Then she ran outside and down the street as fast as she could. She ran to her backyard. To her garden. Then she did what Mary Beth had told her to do.

She yanked a plant out of the soft dirt. On the bottom of the plant, with lots of dirt still on it, was a giant red radish.

"Rat's knees!" Molly said out loud. "No one told me radishes were under the ground! I thought they grew on the branches like little apples!"

Molly went into the house and washed her radish. She popped it into a plastic bag and ran back to Mrs. Peters's house. She was all out of breath when she got there.

The Scouts had finished talking about

good deeds. Now they were drawing and
cutting something out of paper.

Molly waved her plastic bag. "Look!"
She handed the radish to Mrs. Peters.

"Oh, Molly! I wondered why you ran
off so fast," Mrs. Peters said.

"It looks like she got a call from her

garden," said Roger, with a laugh. "An emergency call. Dr. Duff to the rescue!"

Molly frowned at Roger. She would never let Roger know about her big mistake. That she had radishes all the time and never knew it!

Mrs. Peters took the radish out of the bag. "Molly, this is the biggest radish I ever saw."

Kevin gave a long, low whistle. "It's a monster!" he said.

"It's not fair," said Tracy. "Molly's radish was in the ground longer. It had more time to grow."

"Well," said Mrs. Peters, "that was very clever of Molly to let her radishes grow longer. It is the biggest radish in our troop. It may even be a winner at the fair this year. Molly, you have a real green thumb."

Molly beamed. She felt good. Mrs. Peters pinned her badge on her Pee Wee Scout kerchief.

"Molly's radish was the last one," said Mrs. Peters. "But it turned out to be the best one."

Molly sat down beside Mary Beth.

"I wish I'd waited longer to pull mine up," said Mary Beth.

"Please don't tell my secret," said Molly.

"You can always trust a Pee Wee Scout," said Mary Beth, with a smile.

Roger walked over to the girls. "What's the best thing you can put in a pumpkin pie?"

"Pumpkin?" said Mary Beth.

"Your teeth!" said Roger. Then he laughed at his own joke.

Molly didn't mind, though. She was glad to have her new badge.

And she was glad to have friends who were Pee Wee Scouts.

Pee Wee Scout Song

(to the tune of
"Old MacDonald Had a Farm")

Scouts are helpers, Scouts have fun
Pee Wee, Pee Wee Scouts!
We sing and play when work is done,
Pee Wee, Pee Wee Scouts!

With a good deed here,
And an errand there,
Here a hand, there a hand,
Everywhere a good hand.

Scouts are helpers, Scouts have fun,
Pee Wee, Pee Wee Scouts!

☆ Pee Wee Scout Pledge ☆

We love our country
And our home,
Our school and neighbors too.

As Pee Wee Scouts
We pledge our best
In everything we do.